Isabella's Secret

Jane Tanner

PUFFIN BOOKS

Underneath the apple tree,
the grass felt soft as a pillow.
Isabella lay listening to the
friendly sounds around her.

Leaves rustled, a sparrow chirped,
a bee hummed . . .

Hush . . .

What was that?

Two tiny tinkling voices calling:

ʻIsabella . . . Isabella . . .

'Come and play with us.'

Isabella trembled with excitement.
She had always looked for fairies in the garden,
and here they were!

Up she jumped and played with them.

She blew shimmering rainbow bubbles,

as light as fairies' wings.

Her tiny friends gleefully darted and hovered,

fluttered and drifted around her.

Then Isabella showed them her treasures.

Because she loved so many floating, flying things,
the fairies guessed her secret wish.

They had secrets of their own to share,
so they whispered to Isabella:

'Peek very softly, don't make a sound. Come and look
between the leaves, there's magic all around.
There are tiny worlds within your world, and
playmates to be found.'

'Can you see what we see?'

'Come closer . . .'

Suddenly, Isabella felt herself getting
smaller and smaller.

Hooray for fairy dust!

Her wish had come true.

At last she could fly!

How thrilling it was to be so small!

And to see the world as a new
and wondrous place.

She danced with her friends,
twirling and fluttering among the flowers.

Isabella felt so happy and
full of sunshine.
She was as light as thistledown.

But she knew she couldn't
stay little forever.

Isabella felt herself getting
bigger and bigger.

Still keeping the magic in her heart,
she let her feet lightly touch the ground.

'Will you come and play with me again?'
she asked shyly.

In voices like silvery music the fairies answered:

'Tiptoe softly in long grass and smell the flowers
as you pass. Gather leaves as they float by.
Dance with each bright butterfly. Then wait
beneath the apple tree — and call us . . .

'. . . very quietly.'